## DON'T BE MAD, IVY

Ivy would be anybody's favorite friend. She doesn't mind breaking the rules once in a while, especially if it makes the game more fun. She is brave too. She stands up to the neighborhood bully, and she doesn't mind making a total spectacle of herself if it gets the neighbors to invite her over for a swim.

Everyone will recognize parts of themselves in Ivy, and will love spending time in her special world.

"Ivy, a down-to-earth descendant of Haywood's Betsy, Cleary's Ramona and Konigsburg's Jennifer, makes a debut here in six episodes that are bound to strike sympathetic chords in kids.... Ivy is a lively, spunky kid and getting to know her is a pleasure."

—*School Library Journal*

ALSO BY CHRISTINE McDONNELL

*Toad Food and Measle Soup*
*Lucky Charms and Birthday Wishes*
*Count Me In*
*Just for the Summer*

# DON'T BE
# MAD, IVY

# DON'T BE MAD, IVY

by Christine McDonnell

*pictures by Diane de Groat*

*Puffin Books*

*For my father*

PUFFIN BOOKS
Viking Penguin Inc., 40 West 23rd Street, New York, New York 10010, U.S.A.
Penguin Books Ltd, 27 Wrights Lane, London W8 5TZ (Publishing & Editorial) and
Harmondsworth, Middlesex, England (Distribution & Warehouse)
Penguin Books Australia Ltd, Ringwood, Victoria, Australia
Penguin Books Canada Limited, 2801 John Street, Markham, Ontario, Canada L3R 1B4
Penguin Books (N.Z.) Ltd, 182–190 Wairau Road, Auckland 10, New Zealand

First published by Dial Books for Young Readers
Published in Puffin Books 1988
Text copyright © Christine McDonnell, 1981
Illustrations copyright © Diane deGroat, 1981
All rights reserved
Printed in the United States of America
by R. R. Donnelley & Sons Company, Harrisonburg, Virginia

Library of Congress Cataloging-in-Publication Data
McDonnell, Christine.    Don't be mad, Ivy.
Summary: Ivy's world of fun, frustration, and excitement is revealed in six episodes.
[1. Friendship—Fiction]   I. deGroat, Diane, ill.   II. Title.
[PZ7 .M47843Do  1988]    [Fic]    87-7155    ISBN 0-14-032329-5 (pbk.)

# CONTENTS

# THE BIRTHDAY PRESENT

Ivy and her friend Bill were playing in the sandpile at Bill's house. A truck had brought the sand and dumped a big pile in Bill's backyard.

Bill climbed to the top of the sandpile. "Let's pretend this is a mountain," he said to Ivy.

Ivy scrambled up and slid down. Bill slid behind her.

"Let's slide backwards," said Ivy, and they did.

"Let's slide on our stomachs," said Bill, and they did.

"I'm itchy," Ivy said. "I have sand in my sneakers."

"I have sand in my hair," said Bill, shaking his head like a wet dog.

"I have sand down my back," Ivy said, and she jumped up and down to jiggle it out.

When they finished sliding, Ivy and Bill made a town in the sand. Ivy made buildings out of little pieces of stone and wood. Bill planted stick trees around the town. Together they made roads and pushed Bill's little cars all through the town. They made people out of leaves and flowers.

"I'll bring my toy animals over tomorrow," Ivy said.

"I want to build a castle on top," said Bill, "and dig a tunnel, and make a bridge with sticks and string."

"Bill! Bill, it's time to go," his mother called.

"I have to go to my grandmother's," said Bill. "I'll see you tomorrow, Ivy."

Ivy walked home, thinking about the sandpile. "Maybe I can make a town at my house," she said to herself.

She was sitting on the steps in front of her house making a new village out of pebbles and little fir twigs when the mailman came.

"I have a letter for you, Ivy," he said.

He gave Ivy a little envelope. She opened it and took out the card. There was a picture of a boy wearing a party hat. He was blowing out the candles on a cake.

"It looks like a birthday card," Ivy said. "But it's not my birthday."

She opened the card but she could not read it.

Ivy's mother was in the study.

"Mom, read this, please," Ivy said.

Her mother stopped typing.

"Did the mail come?" she asked.

"My mail came," Ivy said.

Ivy's mother read the card out loud. "Please come to a birthday party for Bill on Saturday at three o'clock."

"Well," said Ivy. "I knew it wasn't my birthday."

"No," said her mother. "It's Bill's birthday. We will have to get him a present. Let's go to the store this afternoon."

After lunch Ivy and her mother went downtown shopping. The toy store had a bright red door, and bells jingled when it opened. Inside the store there were large stuffed animals— tigers, elephants, bears, and even a tall giraffe.

There were dolls and dollhouses. Some dolls were big, with real clothes and fancy hairdos. Others were small, with no hair at all. Some dollhouses had windows and stairs. Others were only big enough for mice.

Ivy looked at the puzzles and the trains. She looked at the colored clay and at the building sets. She could not decide what to get for Bill.

Then Ivy noticed the trucks. They were parked on a long shelf. She looked at the dump truck and at the fire engine. She touched the cars on the carrier truck and the little milk bottles on the old-fashioned milk truck. She pushed the school bus back and forth.

Then she saw the bulldozer. It was bright shiny yellow with thick black treads. It could push sand and scoop it up. It could go uphill with those thick treads. It even had a steering wheel that turned around.

Ivy wanted the bulldozer so much that she forgot it was not her birthday. It was Bill's birthday, and the bulldozer was for Bill.

Ivy's mother paid for the bulldozer, and the shopkeeper put it in a box and put the box in a bag. He handed the bag to Ivy.

"Have fun with your truck," he said.

"Oh, it's not for her. It's for her friend," Ivy's mother answered. But Ivy was not listening. She was thinking about the bulldozer.

When they got home, Ivy's mother found wrapping paper, and Ivy sat down to wrap the present. She spread the paper out on the floor and put the box in the middle. She found the scissors and the tape.

Ivy decided to look at the bulldozer once more before she wrapped it. It was so shiny. There was room behind the steering wheel for a little man. Maybe her little rubber gorilla would fit.

Ivy found the little gorilla in her pencil case. He was really an eraser. Sure enough, he fit perfectly behind the wheel. A gorilla driving a bulldozer! Ivy laughed. Maybe she would make him a hat, the kind that construction workers wear. She could make it out of the plastic bubble that she got from the gumball machine.

Suddenly Ivy remembered. The bulldozer was not hers. It was a present for Bill.

Ivy took the gorilla out of the driver's seat and put him in her pocket. She put the bulldozer back in the box. She covered the box with paper and stuck it on with tape. It was wrinkled only on the corners.

Ivy's mother tied a ribbon around the box and made a big bow. Ivy made a card with a picture of herself on it. It said HAPPY BIRTH-

DAY BILL FROM YOUR FRIEND IVY. Ivy's mother put the present and the card on top of the book-case in Ivy's room.

Every day Ivy looked at the present. She tried to remember what the bulldozer looked like. She pretended that it was her birthday and the present was for her.

On Saturday Ivy's father planned to walk her over to Bill's house for the party on his way downtown. Ivy put her jacket on over her new jumper and went downstairs.

"I'm ready, Dad," she said.

Her father took her hand in his and they went out the door and down the steps. Ivy's mother waved good-bye.

"Wait a minute, Ivy," she called. "Where's the birthday present?"

Ivy looked down at the ground. She pushed her toe into the dirt. She did not answer.

"Ivy, come back here and get that present," her mother said in a firm voice.

Ivy walked back up the steps and inside the house. Very slowly she climbed the stairs and walked to her room. There was the present, all wrapped up, sitting on the bookcase. Ivy carried it downstairs. She looked at it sadly.

"I don't want to give it away," she said.

"But, Ivy, this is Bill's present. It's Bill's birthday, not yours," her mother said.

"I don't care," said Ivy. "I want it."

"Ivy, this one is for Bill," her mother told her. "When it's your birthday, maybe you will get one too. But this one is for Bill."

"Well, I hope he will let me play with it," said Ivy.

Ivy and her father walked to Bill's house. Ivy's father carried the present. When they rang the bell, Bill answered the door. Ivy's father handed Bill the present.

"Thanks!" Bill said.

"Ivy, I'll pick you up on my way home," her father told her.

Ivy walked inside. The other children were playing tag. A pile of presents was stacked on the hall table.

He doesn't even need my present, Ivy thought.

At the party the children played musical chairs, hot potato, and pin-the-trunk-on-the-elephant. Ivy won first prize in the elephant game. She pinned the trunk in exactly the right spot.

Ivy opened her prize. It was a package with three tiny trucks in it: a dump truck, a crane, and a steamroller. Ivy began to feel better about Bill's present.

After the games it was time for ice cream and cake. When all the guests were seated at the table, Bill opened his presents. He got a kite, a football sweat shirt, a hat with horns, a jigsaw puzzle, a softball, a water pistol, three books, and a board game. Then he opened Ivy's present.

First Bill picked up the box.

"This is heavy."

Then he shook it back and forth.

"It doesn't rattle. It thumps."

Then he looked at the card, tore off the paper, and opened the box.

"A BULLDOZER! Wow! Just what I wanted. Thanks, Ivy." Bill grinned at Ivy. Ivy smiled back.

After the party was over and Ivy's father had come to walk her home, Bill pulled Ivy over to the corner of the room.

"Thanks for the bulldozer," he said. "I like it a lot."

"You're welcome," Ivy said. "I like my trucks too."

"I know," said Bill. "I wanted to keep those trucks."

Ivy started to laugh. "You did?" she said. "You know what? I wanted to keep the bulldozer!"

"You did?" said Bill. He laughed too. "When you come over tomorrow, bring your prize. We can try out all our trucks in the sandpile."

"Okay," said Ivy happily.

Ivy walked home holding her father's hand in one hand and her three little trucks in the other.

# DON'T BE MAD, IVY

Miss Green stood at the front of the classroom.

"When you have finished practicing your letters, you may go to the game area and play quietly, or you may pick out a book to look at and sit quietly at your desk."

Ivy was practicing *B*'s and *D*'s. She pretended the capital *D* was a big fat man and the capital *B* was his fat wife. She pretended that they were walking down the street, *DB DB DB*. Behind them came their two sons, little *d* and little *b*. Little *b* was a very obedient son and he looked where he was going. Little *d* was the silly son, who insisted on walking backward, *db db db*. Soon Ivy filled up the whole page.

Ivy gave her paper to Miss Green and went to the back of the room. She found the big wooden ark and sat down on the green carpet in the game area. She took the roof off the ark. Inside were wooden animals, two of each except for the few that had been lost: two elephants, two striped tigers, two bears, two lions, two sheep, two tall giraffes, and many more. A little wooden man and a little wooden woman were inside the ark. The man was Noah and the woman was his wife.

Ivy dumped all the figures onto the carpet and put the roof back on the ark. She stood the animals up all around the ark. Very quietly she made all the right noises for the animals.

*"Growl. Grrr, groowl,"* she muttered for the lion and the tiger. *"Baaa. Mooo"* for the sheep and the cow. *"Neigh"* was the quiet whinny of the zebra, which looked like a horse.

Mr. and Mrs. Noah stood by the ark.

"Is it almost finished?" asked Mrs. Noah.

"Almost," said Mr. Noah. "But I have to put in some more nails."

Ivy moved Noah up to the ark and tapped his side against it, pretending to hammer nails.

"I will fix the shutters," said Mrs. Noah.
Ivy jumped her up to the deck of the boat.
"Now it is ready," said Mr. Noah.
Ivy was careful to keep her voice down. Miss
Green said to be very quiet. Usually Noah
would have called out to the animals in a loud
voice, "Come onto my ark or you will drown."

But this time Noah had to be quiet. So he walked up to each animal and whispered, "Come onto the ark. There is going to be a flood."

"Hey, Ivy. What are you playing?"

A big sneaker pushed over the lions and one giraffe.

Oh, no, thought Ivy. It's Loud Leo.

"Hi, Leo," she said. "I am playing Noah's ark."

"How do you play?" asked Leo in a loud voice. "Can I play too?"

Leo smiled at Ivy. Ivy smiled back reluctantly.

"Leo?" Ivy whispered. "Can you whisper?"

"Of course," Leo whispered loudly. "Everyone can whisper."

"Will you whisper if we play?" whispered Ivy.

"Why?" whispered Leo.

"So we don't get in trouble," whispered Ivy.

"Okay," said Leo, but he forgot to whisper.

Up at the front of the classroom Miss Green frowned and put her finger on her lips.

"Leo, there is going to be a flood. We have to

get the animals into the ark," Ivy whispered softly.

"Okay," said Leo, and he picked up a handful of animals and dropped them onto the deck.

"No, not like that!" said Ivy. "They have to come in two by two. They walk up the gangplank. Noah herds them, and they have a nice straight line."

Ivy shook her head at Leo. "Didn't you ever play this before?" she asked.

"No," said Leo. "Why do they come on in a line? Why don't they fight? Hey! Let's make the tiger chase the sheep. The elephant can step on the rabbit. Let's make this more interesting."

"No, Leo! That's not how you play it."

Ivy lined up the animals. Leo shrugged his shoulders and helped her. When they had all the animals on the ark, Leo raised the gangplank.

"Now what happens?" he asked.

"Now the flood comes," said Ivy. "*Whoosh, whoosh.* The rains are pouring down. For forty days and forty nights. *Whoosh, whoosh.* It's a wild and terrible storm."

Ivy rocked the ark back and forth. The animals rattled inside.

"Hey, Ivy. Let's have a real flood," whispered Leo. "We could float the ark in the water table."

Ivy looked over at the science corner. The water table was not being used. The other children were all at the front of the room.

"Okay," she said.

Leo jumped up and ran over to the science corner. There was only a little water in the water table. Leo glanced at the front of the room. Miss Green was helping some children at the blackboard. They were writing their letters in chalk. Miss Green had her back to the science corner.

Leo quietly filled a bucket full of water and poured it into the water table. Now there was enough water for the ark to float.

Ivy put the ark gently in the water. It did float, but it tipped a little to one side.

"Is it still raining?" asked Leo.

"No," said Ivy. "The rain has stopped. Now the animals and Noah come out on deck and look around."

She carefully brought the little animals out of the ark and balanced them on the tilting deck.

"They have to be careful. It is very slippery," Ivy said. "Now Noah comes out and Mrs. Noah. They look at the sky. The sun comes out. Suddenly a beautiful rainbow appears."

"Wow!" said Leo. "I didn't know that."

"Well, it did," said Ivy. "In the book it says that it did."

The ark floated around the water table tilting on its side. Leo was getting bored.

"Now what happens?" he asked.

"They keep on floating for a while."

"Oh."

The ark floated around a little more, with Ivy pushing it.

Suddenly Leo grabbed the tiger.

"*Roar!*" he said, and he pushed the tiger on top of the lion. "*Growl! Rooarr! Grrr. Yipe. Yip! Yip!*"

A fight broke out on the ark. The lion and the elephant were wrestling with the tiger. The little monkey was jumping around them.

There was a lot of yelling and screaming. Then came a big splash.

The animals fell into the water.

Ivy jumped back from the table in surprise.

Leo swirled the water with his hands, making waves and splashing.

"Oh, no!" he said. "They are still fighting in the water. They might drown. Now the tiger has the lion by the throat. Wow! What a fight."

Leo was so excited that he was almost yelling.

"Leo!" said Ivy. "Stop it! You're ruining the game. That's not the way it happened. Besides, you're making everything all wet. We're going to get in trouble!"

Leo did not listen to Ivy's warning. He was having too much fun. He splashed water out of the table and onto the floor.

"Watch out! It's a waterfall," he said. "The elephant is going over the edge."

Leo threw the elephant onto the floor.

Ivy had to laugh. "Oh, no," she said. "The monkey is going over too." Ivy dropped the monkey into the puddle on the floor.

Now Leo and Ivy were both splashing and making the animals fall over the edge of the table. Even Mr. and Mrs. Noah fell out of the ark and floated on the water.

"It's a good thing everything is wood," said Ivy. "Otherwise they would all drown."

She made another big wave, and the ark floated over to the edge of the table. Leo pushed it over the edge.

"And the boat sails down the waterfall," he said.

The ark hit the floor with a loud crash.

Miss Green turned around from the blackboard. She saw the water all over the floor.

"Leo! Ivy! What is going on back there?" she asked as she walked firmly toward them. "What a mess this is! This is not what I meant by playing quietly. You will have to clean up all this water."

Ivy and Leo did not go outside for recess. Instead, they had to mop the floor and dry off all the toys.

At first Ivy was very angry at Leo. She would not talk to him. She sat with her lips pressed together and a scowl on her face as she dried off the little animals.

It's all Leo's fault, she thought.

"Don't be mad, Ivy," said Leo as he mopped the floor.

Ivy did not answer. But as she was drying off the ark she began to giggle. She remembered the elephant going over the waterfall.

"Leo," she said. "I'm not mad anymore. It was a funny game. You play Noah's ark better than my old way."

She laughed. "Remember the fight?"

Leo laughed too. "Remember the way the ark tipped?" he said.

They were finished cleaning before the class came back from recess.

"Leo," Ivy said. "Tomorrow, do you want to play farm with me? I have a good idea."

"What is it?" asked Leo.

"Well, there's this farmyard with a chicken coop. Then this fox comes, and he tries to sneak in and steal the chickens."

"Oh, I get it," said Leo. "And then there's a big fuss."

"Yes. The chickens all squawk and run

around like crazy. They try to escape. But the fox attacks. The chickens' feathers go flying everywhere. It's a mess."

Leo smiled at Ivy. Ivy smiled at Leo.

"We can take turns being the fox," Ivy said.

"Ivy, you're good to play with," said Leo.

"So are you, Leo," said Ivy.

And they put the dry ark back on the shelf.

# THE SWIMMING POOL

"Ivy, go play outside, dear. It's much too nice to stay indoors."

Ivy's mother opened the door and gently pushed Ivy through. The screen banged shut behind her. Ivy dragged the toes of her sandals across the porch floor, making a scraping sound.

It was hot outside. There was nothing to do. Ivy sat down on the lowest porch step and began to draw in the dirt with an old Popsicle stick she found in her pocket. Why did grownups always send kids outside and then stay indoors themselves? What was there to do outside? Her older brother, Jim, was off playing baseball with his friends. He never wanted to play with her anyway. "Beat it, shrimp," he would say. Her older sister, Ann, had gone downtown to buy a new magazine. She never bought magazines that Ivy liked. There were no stories in them, just pictures of clothes.

Ivy wrote her name in the dirt. I V Y. She was sitting and thinking of things to do when she heard the sound of children laughing. It came from around the other side of the house.

Ivy ran around behind the house into the garden. She stood behind a bush at the corner of the house and peeked out.

There was a new swimming pool set up in the yard next door. It was red with blue trim. All the children who had moved in next door were in the pool. They were splashing each other and laughing. They even had a beach ball.

The new neighbors were older than Ivy, but maybe they would invite her into the pool.

Ivy stepped out from behind the bush and stood at the edge of the garden. She hoped someone would notice her and invite her to come over. She was too shy to go over by herself without an invitation.

Ivy waited and waited. She pretended to be smelling the roses. But no one noticed her. She tried to catch a little white butterfly that fluttered by. But no one noticed her.

Ivy wanted to go swimming but she was shy.

Maybe they think I am busy in the garden, Ivy thought. Maybe they think that I don't want to go swimming. Maybe they think that I don't have a bathing suit.

Ivy had a plan. She ran back into the house and up the stairs. In her bottom drawer she found her bathing suit. It smelled salty like the beach. She put it on and ran downstairs in her bare feet. She ran back into the garden and stood looking over at the next yard.

The children next door did not notice her. They went right on splashing and laughing.

Ivy stood watching them for a few minutes.

Maybe they don't know that this is my bathing suit, she thought. Maybe they think it is a leotard.

Ivy pretended she was swimming, just to give her new neighbors another hint. She ran around and around the yard, and moved her arms just like a swimmer. But she looked more like a windmill than a swimmer, and she felt very hot and sticky.

Still the children next door did not notice her.

I bet they think that a bee is chasing me and that's why I'm running around, Ivy thought. I will have to look more like a swimmer.

Ivy looked around the garden. Leaning against the wall of the garage was a long board. Ivy tipped it back and let it fall to the ground. She dragged it into the middle of the garden.

"I will be a fancy diver and this will be my diving board."

Ivy walked to the end of the board and jumped up and down, just like a real diver.

"First a swan dive."

She ran down the board and jumped off the end, holding her arms out. Thud. She landed on the grass.

It must be easier to dive in the water, Ivy thought.

Next she did a twisting dive and twirled in the air. Then she did a backward jump.

Each time, Ivy landed on the grass with a thud.

No one next door noticed her dives.

Maybe they think that I don't like to get wet, Ivy thought as she watched the children playing. Maybe they think I'm afraid of the water.

Ivy ran back inside again.

"Mom, where's my pail?" she yelled.

"Outside, in the garage," her mother answered from upstairs.

Ivy found her pail on a shelf and carried it back to the garden. She filled the pail with water from the hose. Standing at the edge of the garden where everyone could see her, Ivy poured the water over her head. It ran down her face and tickled her back.

But no one was watching.

Ivy was half wet and half dry. She wanted to go swimming.

"I will make them notice me," she said to herself.

In the garage Ivy found her beach toy from last summer. It was a spotted sea monster that fit around her waist. She blew it up and put it on. Then she walked slowly around the garden with the sea monster around her middle.

No one noticed.

I will pretend this is a real monster, Ivy decided.

She put the toy in the middle of the garden and pretended to swim around it, waving her arms in fancy strokes.

"Oh, no! A monster!" she said. She made

pretend splashes in the air. "A monster! Help me. I'm drowning. Help!" Ivy was too shy to yell very loudly.

She looked hopefully over at the pool next door. But still no one called to her. The children had not seen or heard her. They were all yelling and laughing themselves.

Ivy stood with her hands on her hips and stared over at her neighbors. She wanted to go swimming in that new pool and that was that. She did not want to pretend anymore.

This time Ivy was not taking any chances. She put her sea monster around her waist. She turned on the hose and dragged it halfway across the yard. She stood directly across from the new swimming pool. She lifted the hose up over her head and let the water pour all over her. It splashed on her face. It streamed off her shoulders and trickled down her whole body. Ivy looked like a statue in a fountain.

At last her new neighbors noticed her.

"Hi," said the oldest boy.

The others turned around. "Hi," they said.

"Why are you standing under that hose?" asked a tall girl.

"Because I'm hot," Ivy answered.

"Would you like to come swimming?" asked a younger boy with freckles all over his face.

"Yes," said Ivy. "Yes, I would!" She skipped back and turned off the water and put away the hose. Then she ran across the yard and climbed into the pool.

"What's your name?" asked the oldest boy.

"Ivy."

"Next time come over right away," said the tall girl.

"Sure," said the oldest boy. "Don't be shy, Ivy."

Ivy grinned and dunked her head right under the cool water.

# THE BORROWED BEAR

On Saturday afternoon Ivy was playing with her Pick Up Sticks when the phone rang. It was her friend Phyllis.

"Ivy, can you come over to my house and play?" asked Phyllis.

"I'll ask my mother," said Ivy.

Ivy's mother said, "Yes, but wear your rubbers."

So Ivy put on her rubbers and her jacket and walked to Phyllis's house. Phyllis's father was making bread in the kitchen. He was pounding the dough and pushing it over and over on itself.

"If you come back in about two hours, the bread will be finished," he said, "and you may each have a fresh slice while it's hot."

The girls went downstairs to the playroom. An old dollhouse stood on a table in the corner.

"Let's fix up the living room," suggested Phyllis.

She took out a big book of wallpaper samples from the bookcase.

"We will have to pick two that go together because one page isn't big enough for the whole room."

Ivy turned the pages. There were patterns with flowers and some with pinecones. There were baskets of fruit and clumps of vegetables. One page had pink and blue teddy bears and blocks on it.

"But that would look silly in a living room," Ivy said.

Ivy picked out a page of green and yellow stripes. Phyllis picked out a page of orange flowers.

"These look nice together," she said.

Phyllis found the glue and Ivy began to cut the paper. It was hard to get it to fit in the corners.

When they were finished, Phyllis said, "The

walls look fine, but the furniture and the rug look terrible."

Ivy agreed. "Let's make new furniture," she said.

"I'll get my mother's scrap bag," Phyllis said. "You look around for good junk. Things we can use for furniture."

Phyllis went upstairs.

Ivy looked around the playroom. There were shelves stacked with old toys and games, and a toybox filled with baby toys left over from Phyllis's little sister, Amy. In the game boxes Ivy found different-shaped wooden markers that could be used for tables and lamps. In the toybox she found blocks that could become a sofa and a chair. She found pipe cleaners and two little erasers in a cigar box on the shelf. "These are good for lots of things," she said to herself.

Ivy put all her discoveries in front of the dollhouse and looked around again. On the table next to the old couch she saw something else. It was a bear. A funny, furry little bear. He was just a little bit bigger than Ivy's hand.

Ivy picked him up. His arms and legs moved.

He had shiny brown eyes. Ivy made him walk up and down the arm of the couch. He marched like a soldier.

She sat the bear down on the cushion with his legs sticking out in front of him. He did not fall over.

Ivy picked him up and stared at his face. He had a funny little smile.

"Whose bear are you?" she asked him.

He did not answer.

"Are you Phyllis's bear?"

Still no answer.

"Maybe you are Amy's bear," she said. But the bear said nothing.

"I wish you were my bear," Ivy said. "I would make you a cave under my bed. I would give you a red jacket and a wool hat. You could be a lumberjack bear."

Ivy stared hard at the bear.

"Would you like to come home with me?" she asked.

Just then Phyllis came down the stairs with an armful of material. She dumped it on the floor in front of the dollhouse.

"There's some orange towel here that would

make a good rug," she said. She started to cut it to fit.

Ivy picked out some green material. It looked like it had been pajamas. She covered the blocks with it and stuck them together with glue.

"Look. A couch," she said.

But even while Ivy was working on the furniture, she was thinking of the bear.

"Fresh bread. Come and get it," called Phyllis's father.

The girls went upstairs to the kitchen. While they were eating their bread, the phone rang.

"Time to go home, Ivy," said Phyllis's father.

"Okay," said Ivy. "I left my jacket downstairs."

Ivy went down to the playroom by herself. She put on her rubbers and her jacket. She looked at the dollhouse. Then she looked at the bear.

"Maybe no one will miss you," she said, and she put the bear into her pocket. His head stuck out of the opening, but Ivy stuffed a mitten on top of him to cover him up.

"Good-bye, Ivy," said Phyllis as Ivy went out the door.

"Good-bye," called Ivy as she ran down the front walk.

When Ivy got home, she went up to her room. She took the bear out of her pocket and hid him under her pillow. Then she went downstairs and put her jacket away in the hall closet.

After supper she went back to her room. She took out the bear and sat him on her bed.

In her doll's suitcase she found the red jacket. It fit the bear perfectly. But what could she use for a hat? All of her dolls' hats looked silly on a bear. This bear needed a wool hat.

Ivy went downstairs to the front closet and looked on the back shelf. There were lots of old gloves there. She picked out a blue mitten that had no mate and ran upstairs with it.

Ivy found her scissors underneath the pile of cardboard on the shelf of the bookcase. She cut off the thumb of the mitten.

*Clip.*

There it was, a perfect blue wool hat.

Ivy rolled up the edge and put the hat on the bear's head. He looked very handsome.

"All you need now is a pair of boots," said Ivy. She sat and thought for a minute. She did not know where to get boots for a bear.

Ivy stared at the bear. "I think you must be Amy's," she said. "I wonder if she knows you're gone."

Ivy frowned. Having the bear was not as much fun as she had thought it would be. It would be more fun if she could play with him with someone else. Someone like Phyllis. But that was impossible.

Ivy put the bear on top of her bureau. Then she thought again. What if her mother noticed him there? "Whose bear is this?" her mother would say.

Ivy hid the bear in her top drawer.

"Ivy," her mother called. "Time for bed."

"Okay, Mom," Ivy answered.

She put on her pajamas.

I wonder if Amy misses the bear, she thought.

She brushed her teeth and washed her face. She kept on worrying.

"I wonder if Amy sleeps with the bear," Ivy said to herself. She looked sternly at herself in the mirror. What should she do?

Then Ivy had an idea. She walked to the top of the stairs.

"Mom?" she called down the stairs. "Can I call Phyllis? It's very important."

"*May* I call Phyllis," her mother corrected. "Can't it wait until tomorrow?"

"No," said Ivy. "Really."

"Well, all right. But only talk for a second," said her mother.

Ivy used the phone in the upstairs hall. She dialed Phyllis's number. The phone rang three times. Phyllis's mother answered.

"Hello?"

"Hello. May I please speak to Phyllis? This is Ivy."

"Why, Ivy, it is very late to call. Phyllis is getting ready for bed."

"I know, but it's very important, and it will only take a minute," Ivy said.

Phyllis's mother called, "Phyllis!" Then Ivy heard footsteps. Then Phyllis's voice said, "Hello?"

Ivy's throat itched. Her voice trembled. "It's me. Ivy," she said. "You know when I was at your house playing today?"

"Yes," said Phyllis.

"Well, I brought home a bear that was in your playroom. I think he must be Amy's. I wanted to try my doll's jacket on him."

"Is it a little bear?" asked Phyllis.

"Yes. He can move his arms and legs," Ivy said.

"Oh. That's Amy's old bear. She doesn't use it. You can borrow it for a while."

Ivy let out a deep breath. "Thanks, Phyllis," she said.

"Good night. See you tomorrow," said Phyllis.

"Good night," said Ivy.

Ivy went back to her room and took the bear out of the top drawer. She put him on her pillow.

When Ivy's mother came to kiss her good night, she asked Ivy, "Where did you get that nice bear?"

"I borrowed him from Phyllis and Amy," Ivy answered.

Ivy's mother turned off the light. In a little while Ivy fell asleep with the borrowed bear tucked under her arm.

# SLIDING ON ICE

Ivy walked home from school with Bill and Phyllis.

"Let's cut through the park," said Phyllis. "I want to see the big hill."

"My brother said it's covered with ice," said Bill. "You don't even need a sled."

They clumped up the walk into the park. It was not easy to run in rubber boots.

The hill was covered with children sliding on the ice. Some had saucer sleds. Some used pieces of cardboard from large boxes. The hill was slippery and hard with ice frozen solid on top of the snow.

"Look at that big kid," said Ivy. "He's sliding down standing up!" A tall boy with a striped ski hat was sliding down the hill using his feet as skis. He held his arms out to the sides for balance, like a tightrope walker.

"I'm going to slide sitting down," said Ivy.

She climbed slowly up the hill. The ice was slick. Twice she slipped back and had to start again.

"If you step sideways, you won't slip so much," an older girl suggested. "Use the sides of your boots to dig into the crust."

The children slowly climbed up sideways. At last all three stood at the top of the hill.

"It's a long way to the bottom," said Phyllis.

"Come on," said Ivy. "It's just a hill. I'll go first."

"What will you slide on?" Phyllis asked. "You don't have any cardboard and you haven't any saucer."

"I told you already," said Ivy, and she slapped herself on the seat of her green snowsuit.

Ivy sat down on the ice.

"It's cold!" she said. "Gotta go before I freeze my fanny."

She pushed off and began to slide with her

legs straight out in front of her and her arms
pressed close to her sides. She leaned forward.
The air rushed by her face, blowing wet snow
crystals against her skin. Beneath her the icy
hill felt hard and bumpy. She slid all the way
to the bottom, jumped up, and brushed herself
off.

"Come on down," she called to her friends.
Soon all three stood at the bottom of the hill.

"Let's hold hands this time," Phyllis suggested to Ivy as they climbed the hill again.

Ivy and Phyllis held hands and laughed all
the way down. Bill slid down after them.

"Let's make a train," he said.

At the top of the hill they sat in a row with Bill in front, Phyllis in the middle, and Ivy at the end.

"I'm the caboose," Ivy said.

"I'm the engine," said Bill. *"Whooo, whooo!"* He made a whistle sound.

"What am *I*?" asked Phyllis. "I'm squished in the middle."

"You're the peanut butter and jelly," said Ivy, and she started to laugh.

They were all laughing and jiggling so much that they started to slide down the hill without even pushing off.

"Look out, we're moving!" Bill called. "Engine to caboose—hold on."

Ivy held on to Phyllis and Phyllis held on to Bill as they slid down the slick hill.

The train came to a stop at the bottom. Ivy, Phyllis, and Bill were just getting up when Leo came thumping over. He was wearing heavy rubber boots that laced up to his knees. An older boy was with him. They were both pulling sleds.

"Hi," said Leo.

"Hi, Leo," said Ivy.

"This is Ed," said Leo, pointing to the tall boy beside him. "We call him Bulldog on my street."

"Hi," said Ivy.

Bulldog just grunted. He did not say hello.

"Let's go down again," said Bill. "The hill is all ice," he said to Leo. "It's fast. Come on up to the top."

Bill began to sidestep up the hill. Leo started to follow.

"Aw. We don't want to slide on this dinky little hill," said Bulldog. "This is just a gopher hill. Come on, Leo. Let's go."

Bill, Phyllis, and Ivy turned and stared at Leo's friend. He did look a little like a bulldog.

"This is *not* a dinky hill," said Ivy with her hands on her hips. "There are big kids here, much bigger than you!"

"Yeah," said Phyllis, and she pointed to the boy in the striped hat who skied down standing up.

Bulldog grunted. "This is nothing compared to Snake Hill. That's a real hill. This is just for babies. Come on, Leo, let's go."

Snake Hill! Ivy and Bill and Phyllis were

silent for a minute. Snake Hill was the most dangerous hill in town. It was very steep with three sharp curves. Even without ice, it was hard to steer on Snake Hill.

Leo hesitated. He looked up at the top of the park hill. "Let's try this one first," he said to Bulldog.

Bulldog frowned and shook his head. "Not me. I'm going to Snake."

Leo turned to the others. "Come with us. Let's take a look."

Ivy, Bill, and Phyllis glanced at each other. Then Ivy shrugged her shoulders.

"Okay," she said. "I'll come and look. But this hill is fine for me."

"Me too," said Bill. "But I'll come."

Phyllis nodded yes but she looked worried.

The five children walked out of the park and along the road toward Snake Hill. Bulldog walked ahead of the others.

"Come on, Leo," he said over his shoulder.

Leo looked at his friends. He could not decide what to do. "Bulldog is the toughest kid on my block," he explained. "He usually doesn't like younger kids, except me."

He ran to catch up with Bulldog.

At the top of Snake Hill the children stopped and stared at the ice. They could not see beyond the first curve, but they could hear shrieks and yells below.

Bulldog inched his sled out into the middle of the street.

"Come on, Leo," he said.

Leo stayed on the corner with the others.

"Do you think you can steer around corners on ice?" asked Bill.

"Sure," said Bulldog. "What's the matter? You scared?"

Bill did not answer but his face grew pink.

Leo looked down at his big boots.

Ivy spoke up. "We are *not* scared. We're smart! If you're so brave, why don't you go down alone?"

Bulldog ignored her. He kept on staring at Leo.

"What's the matter, Leo? Aren't you coming?"

Leo did not answer.

Bulldog looked at all four children. He spit on the ice.

"See you around, chicken," he said to Leo. "I always knew you were a baby."

Leo kept staring at his feet. He blinked his eyes fast.

Bulldog lay down on his sled, and it started to slide before he even pushed off. He was going very fast. At the first curve his sled skidded off the trail and into a tall hedge.

"Ow!" he yelled as he crashed.

When he saw Bulldog crash, Leo left his sled by the streetlight and inched his way down the slippery hill. The other children followed carefully.

Three older boys climbing back up the hill reached Bulldog first. They helped him up. His lip was bleeding, and one knee of his jeans was torn. His sled was bent from the crash.

Leo picked Bulldog's hat out of the hedge and handed it to him. "Want me to help you get home?" he asked Bulldog.

Bulldog looked at Leo and sneered. "I don't need any baby to help me," he said, pulling his hat down over his forehead. He wiped his lip on the sleeve of his jacket. "Get lost."

Bulldog limped slowly up the hill, dragging

his crooked sled. Leo, Ivy, Bill, and Phyllis watched him go.

"That's the fourth crash today," said one of the older boys. "You kids better stay clear."

Ivy patted Leo on the shoulder. "Let's go back to the park. We can make a really long train now. You can be the caboose this time, Leo."

"Okay," said Leo. "That's what I wanted to do all along." Leo smiled a big grin. He was missing a front tooth.

At the top of the park hill they made another train.

"Ready, Leo?" Ivy asked. "Hang on."

"Toot, toot!" said Phyllis, the engine.

"Clang, clang!" yelled Leo, the caboose.

"All aboard," called Bill.

"Look out below," shouted Ivy as they pushed off.

When they reached the bottom, Leo let go and turned a backward somersault on the icy snow. He came up laughing.

"Let's go again," he said.

They made three more trains.

"It's late," said Phyllis, looking at the sky.

The sun had set, leaving only a rosy glow behind the pine trees at the edge of the park. The streetlights cast yellow circles on the sidewalk.

The four friends walked across the frozen park together and said good-bye at the corner.

"Come with us again tomorrow, Leo," said Ivy.

"You bet," said Leo as he waved good-bye.

# CHRISTMAS EVE

On Christmas Eve Ivy and her family decorated their Christmas tree. They always bought it the day before, on December 23. All three children went with their father to the Christmas tree lot behind the Boys' Club. They looked for a long time before they found a tree that everyone liked.

Jim wanted a very tall tree.

"But it won't fit under the living room ceiling," said Mr. Adams.

Ann wanted a very full tree.

"But it won't fit through the front door," Mr. Adams said.

Ivy wanted a little tree. "No one else will buy it," she explained. "And it will be all alone at Christmas." Ivy had just heard the story of the little fir tree, and she felt sorry for the little tree in the lot.

"But it won't hold all our ornaments," said Mr. Adams. "Someone with a small family and a little house will buy that tree."

Finally Mr. Adams found the perfect tree leaning against the back fence of the lot. It was tall, but not too tall, and full, but not too full.

The tree spent the night on Ivy's front porch with its trunk in a bucket of water. Ivy went out to see it several times before she went to bed.

"Do you miss your forest?" she asked. Of course, she knew the tree would not answer. It did not even move a single branch. "Did you have birds for friends?" Ivy asked, still pretending. She was thinking of the little fir tree with friendly birds sitting on its branches.

"I bet you are cold out here," said Ivy.

Ivy went back inside and rummaged through the front hall closet. She found a long red and black scarf that her father used to wear. She took it outside and wrapped the scarf around the tree branches.

"There. That will keep you warm," she said, and she went upstairs to bed.

The next day Mr. Adams put the tree up in the living room. He screwed the base of the tree into the red and green Christmas tree holder. He strung a piece of wire from the tree to the wall to hold it up.

"How does it look?" he said.

"It tilts to the left," said Ann.

Mr. Adams tightened the wire on the right side.

"Now how does it look?" he asked.

"It leans to the right now," said Jim.

Mr. Adams scowled, but he tightened the wire on the left side.

"It leans back now," said Ann.

"Too bad," said Mr. Adams. "It will have to do." He sounded cross.

Next he untangled the Christmas tree lights and spread them out in a long line on the carpet. When he plugged the lights into the socket to test them, three bulbs did not light up.

"Where are the replacements?" growled Mr. Adams.

Ivy found a spare box of bulbs in the ornament box. Mr. Adams unplugged the lights and screwed in the new bulbs.

"Now this should be perfect," he said as he plugged the lights into the socket once more.

Suddenly there was a *POOF* and all the lights went out.

"It's a fuse," said Jim.

"I *know* it's a fuse," said Mr. Adams through clenched teeth. "Why don't you kids go help Mom with lunch?"

Mrs. Adams changed the fuse while the children made sandwiches. After lunch Ivy and Jim and Ann strung popcorn and cranberries to put on the tree. Three pieces of popcorn, three cranberries, was the pattern. There was a bowl of popcorn to eat too. The kitchen smelled of gingerbread cookies baked to hang on the tree.

Ivy had also made paper chains for the tree and pipe cleaner candy canes—red and white ones twisted together.

It was dark outside by four o'clock.

"The lights are done," said Mr. Adams, looking tired but relieved. "Time to decorate."

Ivy carried the tray of gingerbread men into the living room. Ann carried the chains of popcorn and cranberries. Mrs. Adams brought in a tray of hot cider with cinnamon, and Mr. Adams added rum to the grown-ups' mugs.

The tree stood in front of the living room window. Its branches spread out gracefully. It was big enough to hold all the decorations. Next to the tree was a box of the family ornaments. Jim was unwrapping the shiny balls.

"Be careful," warned Mrs. Adams. "Some of those balls are very old. That heavy green one hung on my mother's tree when she was a little girl."

Each child had a favorite ornament. Ivy liked the wooden rocking horse. Jim liked the crystal snowflake. Ann liked the clear glass ball with the Swiss village inside.

Mr. and Mrs. Adams hung ornaments on the highest branches.

Ivy looked up at the tree and squinted her eyes. All the colored lights came together like a pattern in a kaleidoscope.

After the tree was decorated, the family ate supper. Then Ann and Jim went upstairs to finish wrapping their presents, and Mr. Adams read stories to Ivy.

They sat in the big armchair in the living room. The Christmas tree lights were on, and their reflection shone in the dark window. Ivy leaned her head against her father's shoulder and listened to the story called "The Little Match Girl," and, because she begged for it again, "The Little Fir Tree." Mr. Adams read "The Night Before Christmas," and they sang "Jingle Bells" together.

Ivy had a piggyback ride upstairs.

"Oof! You are getting too heavy for this, young lady," said Mr. Adams.

He tucked Ivy into bed, and both her parents kissed her good night.

After her parents went downstairs, Ivy lay in bed with her eyes wide open. Ann and Jim were still up. She could hear them talking and laughing softly downstairs.

Ivy was still awake when Ann came upstairs.

Ann put on her nightgown and climbed into bed.

"If you close your eyes and go to sleep, the morning will come faster," she said to Ivy.

Ivy closed her eyes but she did not fall asleep. She kept her eyes closed for as long as she could.

"Ann?" she said.

"Uh-huh," Ann murmured from underneath her quilt.

"Is it almost morning?"

"No. It's still night. Now, go to sleep." Ann rolled over on her side and pulled her quilt up to her chin.

Ivy lay awake in the darkness. It felt like a long time.

"Ann?" she asked again.

Ann grunted from her bed.

"Is it time to get up yet?" Ivy wanted to run downstairs and open all her presents.

"No, it's not morning. Now, go to sleep," said Ann.

"I can't," said Ivy.

"You have to," said Ann.

"I can't," said Ivy.

Ann sat up in bed. "Ivy, you are driving me crazy. Every time I am almost asleep, you ask me if it's time to get up. Now, be quiet and let me sleep."

Ivy bit her lip. She did not mean to make Ann angry. She lay quietly in bed, rubbing the smooth satin edge of her blanket.

Ann burrowed down in her bed and pulled her quilt up around her ears.

"Good night, Ivy," she said from deep inside her covers.

"Good night," said Ivy, feeling lonely.

Ivy lay in bed for a long time. She heard her parents come up the stairs to bed. Then all the house was quiet.

Ivy was still awake. She tossed to the right

and she rolled to the left. But she could not fall asleep.

Maybe it's morning now, Ivy thought.

She looked over at Ann. Ann was sleeping soundly. She did not look ready to get up.

If I wake her up now, and it isn't morning, she'll be angry, Ivy thought. But how will I know when it *is* morning?

Then Ivy remembered the morning star. If the morning star was in the sky, it would be time to get up. Ivy climbed out of bed and stood at the window. The sky was deep blue with tiny stars like pinpricks of light. The moon was out, a white half-circle hanging between the pine trees. But there was no sign of the morning star.

Ivy's bare feet felt so cold that she was afraid they were beginning to freeze. She leaned her elbows on the windowsill and kept her eyes on the sky. Still no sign of the morning star.

Ann's breathing was slow and deep.

I bet she is cozy and warm, thought Ivy.

She imagined her own bed. My bed is soft

and warm, not hard and icy like this floor, she thought.

Ivy looked at the sky again. There was still no sign of the morning star, but she was tired of waiting.

Ivy climbed back into bed. She rubbed her feet back and forth until they were warm. She pulled the covers around herself like a cocoon. Her pillow was cool against her cheek. She rolled up in a little ball and closed her eyes.

"Ivy! Time to get up!" Ann was shaking her.

Ivy woke up. The room was gray in the dawn light.

"Is it morning?" she asked.

"Yes. Merry Christmas! Hurry, it's time to go downstairs," Ann said in a rush. "Put on your slippers and your robe."

Ivy followed Ann out to the hall. Jim stood at the top of the stairs.

"What a bunch of slowpokes," he complained. "What's keeping everyone?"

Just then Mr. and Mrs. Adams came out of their room. Mrs. Adams tied her plaid bathrobe snugly around herself.

"*Brrr*. It's early," she said. "Merry Christmas, everyone."

She gave each of them a hug.

"Let's go!" said Jim.

"Me first," said Mr. Adams. "You children come down when I say ready."

He went down the stairs with his slippers flopping on every step, and disappeared into the living room.

"Ready!" he called.

The children came rushing down the stairs. Ivy was the last one into the room.

The first thing that Ivy saw was the Christmas tree, all lit up in the dark room. The colored lights shone through the branches, and the tinsel sparkled. The ornaments glittered as they swung gently on the tree. The room smelled faintly of sweet sharp pine.

Ivy looked up. A bright silver star with a white light glowed on the very top of the tree. It was a Christmas morning star.

Ivy looked at the bottom of the tree. Standing in front was a blue two-wheel bicycle. It was too small for Ann or Jim. It had a red basket and a shiny silver bell.

"Merry Christmas!" said Ivy's parents.

"Merry Christmas!" said Ivy as she climbed up on her bike.

## Christine McDonnell

grew up near New York City, the youngest of four children. She was graduated from Barnard College and Columbia University School of Library Service. She has worked as a children's librarian in the New York Public Library and as a school librarian in a large junior high school. Currently she teaches at the Center for the Study of Children's Literature, Simmons College. Ms. McDonnell lives in Boston with her husband, who is a painter, and her nine-year-old stepson. This is her first book.


## Diane deGroat

is the illustrator of many books for children, including *The Twins Strike Back* (Dial) and *Little Rabbit's Loose Tooth*, which won the 1978 California Young Reader's Medal. Ms. deGroat was born in New Jersey and received her Bachelor of Fine Arts degree from Pratt Institute. She currently lives in Yonkers, New York, with her husband and daughter.